3.3

Appoquinimir
651 North Bro
Middletown,
D1489424

The Fox and the Stork

RETOLD AND ILLUSTRATED BY GRAHAM PERCY

For Noah

Distributed in the United States of America by
The Child's World®
1980 Lookout Drive • Mankato, MN 56003-1705
800-599-READ • www.childsworld.com

ACKNOWLEDGMENTS
The Child's World®: Mary Berendes, Publishing Director
The Design Lab: Kathleen Petelinsek, Art Direction and Design;
Anna Petelinsek, Page Production

LIBRARY OF CONGRESS CATALOGING-IN-PUBLICATION DATA
Percy, Graham.
 The fox and the stork / retold and illustrated by Graham Percy.
    p. cm. — (Aesop's fables)
 Summary: When sly Mr. Fox invites hungry Miss Stork to lunch but tricks
her out of her portion, she devises a way to get the last laugh.
  ISBN 978-1-60253-200-7 (lib. bound : alk. paper)
 [1. Fables. 2. Folklore.] I. Aesop. II. Title.
 PZ8.2.P435Fr 2009
 398.2—dc22
 [E]   2009001584

Treat others as you would want to be treated.

There once was a sly fox who liked to play tricks on his friends. One day, he thought of a trick to play on Miss Stork. The fox carefully wrote her an invitation to dinner that night.

Miss Stork was very happy to get the invitation. She had never been to Mr. Fox's house before.

"How kind of him," she thought. She quickly went to buy a new dress to wear.

That night, Miss Stork was
all dressed up. Her feathers were
sleek and shiny. She happily
knocked on Mr. Fox's door.

"Come in, come in!" smiled
Mr. Fox. "Dinner is ready."

Miss Stork sat down at the table. She was very hungry and something smelled wonderful. Just then, Mr. Fox brought in two bowls of steaming soup. Miss Stork's mouth began to water.

Mr. Fox hungrily drank
the steaming soup from his
own bowl. But poor Miss
Stork couldn't drink a single
mouthful. Her narrow beak was
too long for the shallow bowl.

Mr. Fox looked up from his empty bowl. He saw that Miss Stork hadn't even touched her soup.

"I'm so sorry you don't like my fine cooking!" he said with a sly, greedy grin. "Let me help you."

And in no time at all, Mr. Fox gulped down Miss Stork's soup as well.

Miss Stork was angry at Mr. Fox's trick, but she didn't show it. Instead, she smiled sweetly.

"Mr. Fox," she said, "you have been so kind. Please join me for dinner at my house next week."

Then she flew home, very hungry indeed.

The following week, Mr. Fox
went to dinner at Miss Stork's
house. He wore his best clothes
and his shiniest shoes. He carried
a large bunch of stolen red roses.

"Come in!" smiled Miss Stork. "I'm afraid dinner is not quite ready. Please join me in the kitchen while I put the finishing touches on it."

Mr. Fox followed Miss Stork to the kitchen. He watched while she finished chopping, mixing, and stirring her soup. It smelled wonderful. The fox licked his lips.

"All ready now," said Miss Stork brightly. She poured the soup into two tall, thin jars.

Miss Stork easily dipped her beak into one jar and drank up all her soup.

But the hungry fox couldn't reach a single drop. His nose was far too short and stubby.

"I'm so sorry you don't like my fine cooking," said Miss Stork, just as Mr. Fox had said to her the week before. "Let me help you."

The hungry fox watched as Miss Stork drank up all his soup as well.

As Mr. Fox said good-bye to Miss Stork, she smiled her sweetest smile.

"Thank you so much for coming," she said, "but do remember—if you play tricks on other people, they might play tricks on you. Always treat others as you want to be treated. Good night."

AESOP

Aesop was a storyteller who lived more than 2,500 years ago. He lived so long ago, there isn't much information about him. Most people believe Aesop was a slave who lived in the area around the Mediterranean Sea—probably in or near the country of Greece.

Aesop's fables are known in almost every culture in the world, in almost every language. His fables are even *part* of some languages! Some common phrases come from Aesop's fables, such as "sour grapes" and "Don't count your chickens before they're hatched."

ABOUT FABLES

Fables are one of the oldest forms of stories. They are often short and funny, and have animals as the main characters. These animals act like people. Often, fables teach the reader a lesson. This is called a *moral*. A moral might teach right from wrong, or show how to act in good, kind ways. A moral might show what happens when someone makes a poor decision. Fables teach us how to live wisely.

ABOUT THE ILLUSTRATOR

Graham Percy was a famous illustrator of more than one hundred books. He was born and raised in New Zealand. He first studied art at the Elam School of Art in New Zealand and then moved to London, England, to study at the Royal College of Art.

Mr. Percy especially loved to draw animals, many types of which can be found in his books. He illustrated books on everything from mysteries to lullabies. He was even a designer for the animated film "Hugo the Hippo." Mr. Percy lived most of his life in London.